This Walker book belongs to:

_____

_____

_____

In praise of loving fathers, especially Curtis,
Steven, Joe and Unk John
K. B.

First published 2010 by Walker Books Ltd
87 Vauxhall Walk, London SE11 5HJ

This edition published 2012

2 4 6 8 10 9 7 5 3 1

Text © 2010 Kelly Bennett
Illustrations © 2010 Paul Meisel

The right of Kelly Bennett and Paul Meisel to be identified as author and
illustrator respectively of this work has been asserted by them in accordance
with the Copyright, Designs and Patents Act 1988

This book has been typeset in Malonia Voigo

Printed in China

British Library Cataloguing in Publication Data:
a catalogue record for this book is available from the British Library

ISBN 978-1-4063-3207-0

www.walker.co.uk

My Dads

Kelly Bennett

illustrated by Paul Meisel

WALKER BOOKS
AND SUBSIDIARIES
LONDON · BOSTON · SYDNEY · AUCKLAND

I have two fathers.

I call this one Dad,

and this one Pa.

To meet them, you'd think Dad and Pa were as different as two fathers could be.

Pa is bald.

Dad is not.

Dad is tall.

Pa is not.

Pa wears boots.

Dad wears suits.

Pa takes
pictures.

Dad takes naps.

Dad's into gadgets.

Pa's into plants.

Dad likes to fish.

Pa *is* a fish.

Dad and I
play sports.

Pa and I
play games.

Pa and I swap stories.

Dad and I swap jokes.

Dad teaches me to cook.

So does Pa.

Pa teaches me to paint.

So does Dad.

Dad loves music.

So does Pa.

Pa loves biking.

So does Dad.

They both help me.

They both cheer me.

In some ways Dad and Pa
are as different as can be.
But in the most important way
they are exactly the same –

they both

Dad and me.

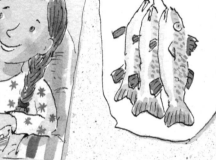

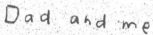

GLUE STICK

love me!

Pa and me.

Kelly Bennett is the author of many books
for children. She divides her time between Texas,
USA, and Jakarta, Indonesia.

Paul Meisel is the illustrator of *Harriet's Had Enough*,
written by Elissa Haden Guest, and *What's the Matter
in Mr Whiskers' Room?* by Michael Elsohn Ross, among
many other books. He lives in Connecticut, USA.

Also by Kelly Bennett:

NOT NORMAN
A Goldfish Story

Kelly Bennett   illustrated by Noah Z. Jones

ISBN 978-1-84428-288-3

Available from all good booksellers

www.walker.co.uk